This Little Tiger book belongs to:

_____

_____

_____

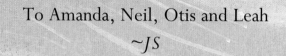

To Amanda, Neil, Otis and Leah
~*JS*

For my good friends
Jim and Raechele
~*TW*

LITTLE TIGER
An imprint of Little Tiger Press Limited
1 Coda Studios, 189 Munster Road, London SW6 6AW
Imported into the EEA by Penguin Random House Ireland,
Morrison Chambers, 32 Nassau Street, Dublin D02 YH68
www.littletiger.co.uk

First published in Great Britain 2002
This edition published 2019

ISBN 978-1-78881-643-4
Printed in China
LTP/1400/5139/0523
6 8 10 9 7 5

Careful, Santa!

Julie Sykes   Tim Warnes

LiTTLE TiGER

LONDON

It was Christmas Eve, and Santa was loading presents on to his sleigh. Santa's little mouse was helping too.

WHOOSH!

A gust of wind blew Santa's beard straight in his face.

"Ho, ho, ho!" he chuckled. "I can't see what I'm doing!"

"Careful, Santa!" warned Santa's cat. "You mustn't lose that sack of presents."

"That would never do!"
Santa agreed, as he carefully
stowed everything away.

Santa helped his little mouse climb aboard
the sleigh.

"Hold on tight!" he boomed. "We're off!"

It was a wild and windy night.

"Oooh my!" shouted Santa, as the sleigh
rocked this way and that. Suddenly, the sack
of presents began to move.

"Careful, Santa!" called Santa's little mouse.
"Mind that sack!"

But Santa wasn't quick enough. The sack slid
across the sleigh and toppled overboard.
"Stop!" cried Santa in alarm. "Down, Reindeer,
down! I've lost all the presents!"

The reindeer struggled
against the wind . . .

. . . and landed as gently as they could.

"Careful, Santa!" they shouted, but
it was too late . . .

"WHOOPS!" cried Santa, landing
on his bottom.

Santa scrambled to his feet.
The presents were scattered far and
wide and he hurried to pick them up.
He didn't notice the frozen pond . . .

"*WHEEEEEE!*" cried Santa,
as he slid across the ice towards
the duckhouse.

"Careful, Santa!" quacked the ducks.
"You nearly squashed us."

"How awful," said Santa as he gathered
up the presents. "Sorry about that.
Has anyone seen my sack?"

"Here it is!" chattered a squirrel from high in a tree. Santa bravely climbed up, but before he knew it he was well and truly stuck.

"Oooh, help!" he cried.

"Careful, Santa!"
called the squirrel.
"I am trying to
be careful," said Santa,
as he struggled to get free.
Very, very slowly, Santa
climbed back down again,
dropping some presents as
he went.

In the playground, a few presents were lying under the swings. Santa put them into his sack, then he spotted some more on the slide.

"Whooooooosh!" cried Santa, as he whizzed down the slide.
  "Careful, Santa, you're going too fast!" warned Santa's cat.
  "Eeek! I can't stop!" said Santa, as he zoomed towards
the snowman . . .

"Sorry, Snowman, I didn't mean to bump you," Santa said, as he dusted himself down and popped the last of the presents into his sack.

"That's it!" he boomed. "It's time to deliver
these presents. Ready, Mouse?"
But where was Mouse? Santa
couldn't see her anywhere.
"Oh dear!" he cried in alarm.
"First I lose my sack of presents,
and now I've lost my little mouse.
This will never do."

The ducks, the squirrel and Santa's cat all crowded round.
"Don't worry, Santa!" they chattered. "She
can't have gone far. We'll help you look for her."

Everyone looked for Mouse.
She wasn't in the duckhouse
and she wasn't at the swings.

She wasn't near the slide or
behind the snowman. Just then,
Santa heard a familiar squeak.
He shone his torch upwards . . .

. . . and there was Mouse, hanging from a branch in a tree.
"Careful!" warned Santa. "It's far too windy to play
up there. That branch doesn't look too safe to me."

But Mouse
wasn't playing.
"I'm stuck," she
squeaked. "Please
get me down!"
Quickly, Santa took off
his jacket and spread it out
on the ground. Everyone
gathered round and held
the coat like a trampoline.
"Hold on tight, everyone, and
don't let go!" said Santa.

"Ready, Mouse?
One, two, three . . .

JUMP!"

Mouse jumped and, with a bounce and a plop,
landed safely on Santa's coat.
"Hooray!" cheered Santa. "Thank you, everyone."

It was time to go. Santa and Mouse hurried aboard their sleigh.

"Reindeer, up, up and away!" cried Santa. WHOOSH! blew the wind.

"Careful, Santa," called everyone,
as the sleigh rocked this way and that.
"Look after that mouse, and HOLD
ON TIGHT TO THAT SACK!"